Christmas for a Kitten

Written by *Robin Pulver*

Paintings by *Layne Johnson*

SCHOLASTIC INC.
New York Toronto London Auckland Sydney
Mexico City New Delhi Hong Kong Buenos Aires

*For families everywhere who share
loving homes with their pets. —R.P.*

For my beloved Sondra. —L.J.

ISBN-13: 978-0-439-89580-4
ISBN-10: 0-439-89580-4

Text copyright © 2003 by Robin Pulver.
Illustrations copyright © 2003 by Layne Johnson.
All rights reserved. Published by Scholastic Inc., 557 Broadway,
New York, NY 10012, by arrangement with Albert Whitman &
Company. SCHOLASTIC and associated logos are trademarks
and/or registered trademarks of Scholastic Inc.

12 11 10 9 8 7 6 5 4 3 2   7 8 9 10 11 12/0

Printed in the U.S.A.   08

This edition first printing, December 2007

The paintings are rendered in oil on Arches watercolor paper.

The design is by Carol Gildar.

On a chilly night, in a barn far, far away from the North Pole,
a kitten that had never seen or heard of Christmas slept snug
against his mother.

Suddenly the kitten was jostled awake, lifted away, and stuffed into darkness. His kitten claws were useless against the big gloved hand. His kitten mews were muffled in the rough cloth sack.

"Too many cats," a cruel voice said as the kitten in the sack was plopped down hard. A door slammed. A motor coughed. Then came a scary, jouncy, rumbling ride. A squealing stop. The kitten felt himself flung through the air. He landed with a bruising thud.

The kitten clawed his way out of the sack. Then he ran and ran to escape the hard road and the terrifying wheels that roared past. He came to a wooded hillside and crawled into a hollow log.

After a long, lonely night, the kitten remembered the lessons his mother had taught him about hunting. The chasing and batting games he used to play were serious business now. If he didn't find food, he would starve.

Sometimes his night hunting took him near houses. Their windows of warm light filled him with longing.

One cold day, people came in a car to the hillside. The kitten watched from his hollow log as they measured trees with their arms, sniffed the branches, and called out to each other.

The kitten ran to the car and leaped up. He peered into a dark, yawning space. It looked warm. He jumped down and squeezed into the farthest corner.

WHACK! WHACK! WHACK! What was that noise?

BOOMF! Something rammed into the space where the kitten crouched. A tree? The strong scent made him sneeze. "Meow-choo!"

Prickly branches crowded him. Then the kitten was off on another jouncy, rumbling ride, in scary darkness again.

Finally the car stopped. The tree was pulled out and away. When no one was looking, the kitten jumped to the ground. The people left the door open long enough. The kitten scooted inside and found a hiding place.

Just in time!

Gr-r-r-r-owf! Rowf! Rowf!

"What's the matter with Barker?" said
a voice. "What's he seeing under that chair?"

Huge nostrils snuffled as the kitten
tried to squeeze out of reach.

"Nothing," said another voice. "Too
much excitement. I'll put him in the bedroom."

The barking nostrils disappeared, but
the kitten couldn't stop trembling.

The frightened kitten watched the people stand the tree up straight. They hung shimmery objects from the branches.

Then the family went into another room. Food smells and eating sounds made the kitten's hungry stomach grumble.

When the people came back, they put small round things and a glass of something white on a table near the tree. The children hung long red things over a big black hole in the wall. Then the family disappeared, calling out, "Leave a light on for Santa!" "No peeking!"

After a long time, the kitten crept out from
his hiding place. Curious, he leapt up on the table, then
dipped his paw into the glass and licked. Meow-yum!
The taste reminded him of his mother. He dipped and
licked, dipped and licked, then chomped into the small
round things nearby. Crunchy! Crumbly!

The kitten stared at the dangling objects on the tree.
His tail twitched until he could stay still no longer.

He leaped,

batted,

chased,

pounced,

attacked.

Suddenly . . . more snuffling . . .
The dog was coming back!
The kitten scrambled to the top of the tree.
Barker followed his nose to leftover crumbs,
slobbering them up.
Finally, a voice called Barker away.
The kitten clung to a high branch, shaking.

Then he heard more sounds:

A noisy clattering from overhead.

Shuffling and huffing from up
inside the big black hole where the long
things hung.

A deep voice grumbling, "Hmmph!
Next year, I'll stick to my diet. Ooof!"

Boots dropped into view, then legs,
finally the strangest, scariest human
being the kitten had ever seen. He saw
a sack . . . then gloved hands—like the
big gloved hands and the sack that had
taken him away from his mother!

The tree swayed, about to fall.
"Mmmmmmmmrrrorow!"
The strange person whirled
and caught the tree.

"What's this? You scared me
out of my boots! Why would
you want to frighten old Santa?"

Santa took a long look around.
"Ho, ho, I see! Milk and cookies
gone. Tree a mess. A brave young
kitten that doesn't belong here. Is
that your problem, puss, you don't
belong anywhere? You can't stay
here, you know. This family *loves* its
cat-chasing dog."

In a twinkling, Santa righted the tree.
He reached into his sack and stuffed the
long red things full. He piled other things
near the tree.

He returned dangly objects to the
branches.

Then Santa scooped the kitten up with
his big gloved hands. But did he stuff him
into the sack as the kitten feared? No!
"Hold on tight!" said Santa, and they
whooshed up through the dark hole,
up, up to the outdoor night.

The kitten saw animals like the
deer he knew from the woods. Santa
told them, "We have a new friend. I'm
going to call him Christmas Cookie,
since he ate mine.
    "All aboard!" said Santa.
"You sit here, Cookie, next to me."

Then the kitten had the ride of his life.
No jounces, no rumbling, no dark scary times.
A smooth sail through a star-bright sky, with
ever so many rooftop landings.

Finally, at dawn, came a long,
long flight to a cold, cold place,
where a house with windows of
warm light waited.

"Welcome home," said Santa.
And he carried the kitten inside.